HELLO, I'M THEA!

I'm *Geronimo Stilton*'s sister. As I'm sure you know from my brother's bestselling novels, I'm a special correspondent for *The Rodent's Gazette*, Mouse Island's most famouse newspaper. Unlike my 'fraidy mouse brother, I absolutely adore traveling, having adventures, and meeting rodents from all around the world!

The adventure I want to tell you about begins at Mouseford Academy, the school I went to when I was a young mouseling. I had such a great experience there as a student that I came back to teach a journalism class.

When I returned as a grown mouse, I met five really special students: Colette, Nicky, Pamela, Paulina, and Violet. You could hardly imagine five more different mouselings, but they became great friends right away. And they liked me so much that they decided to name their group after me: the Thea Sisters! I was so touched by that, I decided to write about their adventures. So turn the page to read a fabumouse adventure about the

THEA SIST

nicky

Name: Nicky
Nickname: Nic
Home: Australia
Secret ambition: Wants to be an ecologist.
Loves: Open spaces and nature.
Strengths: She is always in a good mood, as long as she's outdoors!
Weaknesses: She can't sit still!
Secret: Nicky is claustrophobic — she can't stand being in small, tight places.

Nicky

COLETTE

Name: Colette
Nickname: It's Colette, please. (She can't stand nicknames.)
Home: France
Secret ambition: Colette is very particular about her appearance. She wants to be a fashion writer.
Loves: The color pink.
Strengths: She's energetic and full of great ideas.
Weaknesses: She's always late!
Secret: To relax, there's nothing Colette likes more than a manicure and pedicure.

Colette

Name: Violet
Nickname: Vi
Home: China
Secret ambition: Wants to become a great violinist.
Loves: Books! She is a real intellectual, just like my brother, Geronimo.
Strengths: She's detail-oriented and always open to new things.
Weaknesses: She is a bit sensitive and can't stand being teased. And if she doesn't get enough sleep, she can be a real grouch!
Secret: She likes to unwind by listening to classical music and drinking green tea.

PAULINA

Name: Paulina
Nickname: Polly
Home: Peru
Secret ambition: Wants to be a scientist.
Loves: Traveling and meeting people from all over the world. She is also very close to her sister, Maria.
Strengths: Loves helping other rodents.
Weaknesses: She's shy and can be a bit clumsy.
Secret: She is a computer genius!

Name: Pamela
Nickname: Pam
Home: Tanzania
Secret ambition: Wants to become a sports journalist or a car mechanic.
Loves: Pizza, pizza, and more pizza! She'd eat pizza for breakfast if she could.
Strengths: She is a peacemaker. She can't stand arguments.
Weaknesses: She is very impulsive.
Secret: Give her a screwdriver and any mechanical problem will be solved!

Pamela

Geronimo Stilton

Thea Stilton AND THE MISSING MYTH

Scholastic Inc.

ISBN 978-0-545-65601-6

Based on an original idea by Elisabetta Dami.

www.geronimostilton.com

Published by Scholastic Inc., 557 Broadway, New York, NY 10012.

Text by Thea Stilton
Original title *I segreti dell'Olimpo*
Cover by Giuseppe Facciotto (design) and Flavio Ferron (color)
Illustrations by Barbara Pellizzari and Chiara Balleello (design), Valeria Cairoli (base color), and Daniele Verzini (color)
Graphics by Elena Dael Maso

Special thanks to Beth Dunfey
Translated by Emily Clement
Interior design by Kay Petronio

12 11 10 9 8 7 6 5 4 3 2 1 14 15 16 17 18 19/0

Printed in the U.S.A. 40
First printing, December 2014

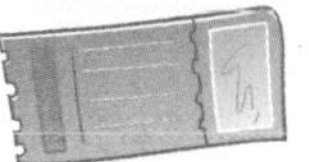

A SPECIAL INVITATION

That Saturday morning, I woke up feeling more CHEERFUL than a chipmunk. I was about to scurry off on a trip that was really SPECIAL, even for a **world traveler** like me!

After a quick ***breakfast***, I checked to make sure I had everything I needed in my ***suitcase***. Then I rushed out on one last errand.

Oh, pardon me, I almost forgot to **INTRODUCE** myself! My

name is **THEA STILTON**, and I am a special correspondent for *The Rodent's Gazette,* Mouse Island's biggest newspaper.

Now, where was I? Oh yes, hurrying over to the **Squeaky-Clean Dry Cleaning Shop**.

The shop owner, Toni Tidytail, greeted me with a **SMILE**. "Hi, Thea! Are you here for your gown? I'll get it for you right away."

Toni disappeared behind a rack of **MULTICOLORED** garments. A few moments later, she reappeared with my dark red evening gown in her paws. It was perfectly pressed.

Toni carefully wrapped the gown in tissue paper. "What a **marvemouse** dress! Are you wearing it for a special occasion?"

I nodded. "I've been invited to a *theatrical performance* on Whale Island."

"Really? What is it — an opera? Or a ballet? I just love the ballet!" cried Toni,

I'm going to a theatrical performance!
Really? A ballet?

doing a quick **TWO-STEP**.

I **smiled**. "Actually, no. It's a GREEK TRAGEDY!"

Toni's snout dropped. "Really? How unusual!"

"Yes, the play is very old. It was written around **two thousand five hundred years ago**!"

Toni was intrigued. "OOH . . . tell me more."

"My friends the THEA SISTERS invited me," I explained. "They recently visited **Greece**."

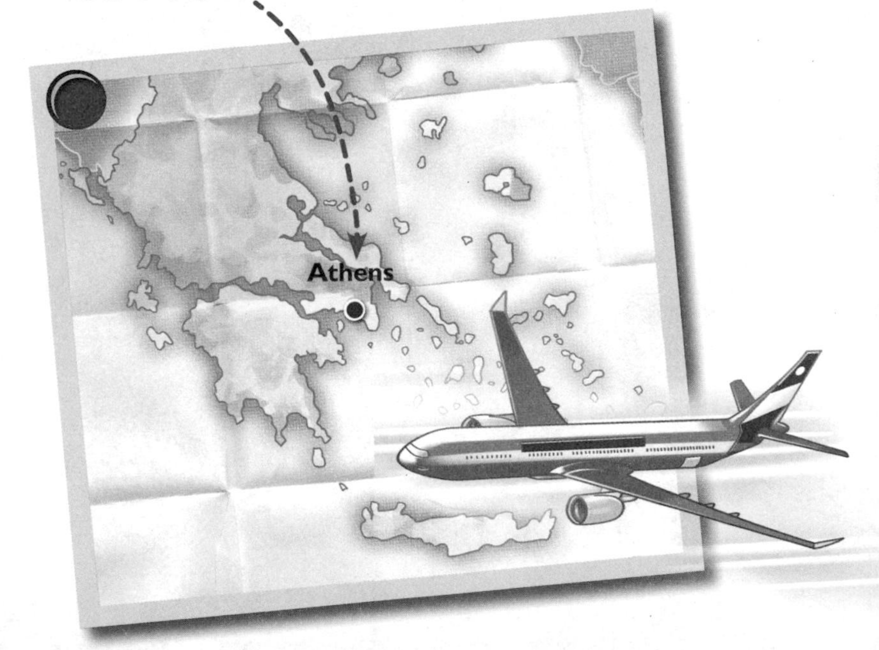

A few years ago, I'd returned to Mouseford Academy, my old school, to teach a journalism class. Colette, Nicky, PAMELA, PAULINA, and **Violet** — the THEA SISTERS — were my star students.

"I should've known those DARLING mouselets were involved!" Toni exclaimed. "I've heard you squeak of them so many times. Were they in Greece on vacation?"

"Yes, a very unusual vacation," I replied. "Full of surprises . . . and MYSTERY!"

Toni's eyes widened. "MYSTERY? What sort of mystery?"

I checked my watch. I still had a few hours before my flight took off for Whale Island. I had just enough time to tell my old friend about the Thea Sisters' latest adventure . . .

WELCOME TO GREECE!

Colette, Nicky, Violet, Pam, and Paulina were **scampering** along a sunlit street filled with shops and restaurants.

"How about a little **lunch**?" said Pam, dragging her paws. "We deserve it after this hike!"

"Come on, it's just a **FEW MORE STEPS**. Our hotel is close — I swear it on a stack of cheese slices!" said Nicky, checking the map of **ATHENS** she held in her paws.

"Are you sure?" sighed Colette, who was pulling an enormouse pink **suitcase** behind her. "You said the same thing half an hour ago!"

"Maybe we're lost," Violet said.

Nicky looked up. "Nope! There it is!"

The mouselets headed for a small white building with bright pink bougainvillea* growing over the front door.

A rodent with a kind snout was setting a small table out front. "Hello! You're the mouselets from Whale Island, right?"

Before the Thea Sisters could answer, the rodent continued squeaking. "I'm Kostantina, the owner of this hotel. Welcome to ATHENS! You're sure to love it here!"

"Thanks," said Paulina, smiling.

Colette started dragging her huge suitcase toward the entrance, hobbling and panting as she went. Kostantina rushed to help her, chattering all the while.

"You're staying for just two nights, right?

* *Bougainvillea* is a tropical shrub or vine with brightly colored flowers.

Welcome to Athens!

You must head straight to the **Acropolis***, if you're not too tired! The view of the city from there is **unforgettable**. I just know you're going to love it."

The mouselets exchanged a **LOOK**. Paulina whispered, "She reminds me of Professor de Mousus when he gives his annual welcome speech, the one that —"

"— never ends!" Pam finished, giggling.

"You'll definitely like the **room** I've prepared for you — it's the biggest one!" the **HOTEL** owner continued. "Now, kick back your paws for a bit, and when you're ready, a **traditional Greek meal** will be waiting for you on the terrace."

Pam perked up at those words. An hour later, she was the first to ***SCURRY*** back downstairs, with her friends trailing behind.

The sunset painted the sky warm **SHADES**

* An *acropolis* is the highest part of an ancient Greek city, where the most important religious and government buildings were located. The Athens Acropolis is a UNESCO World Heritage site.

GREECE

OFFICIAL NAME: Hellenic Republic
CAPITAL: Athens
POPULATION: 10,893,000
SURFACE AREA: 50,949 square miles
OFFICIAL LANGUAGE: Greek

Greece is located in southern Europe, on the Balkan Peninsula. About one-fifth of its territory is made up of islands: There are more than two thousand in all, and most of them are uninhabited!

Greece is rich in history and culture. It's famous for important philosophers such as Socrates, Plato, and Aristotle, and for great masters of literature, theater, mathematics, and medicine. The Olympic Games were born in ancient Greece.

of pink. As they relaxed on the terrace, the mouselets grinned at one another. Their vacation had finally begun!

"I'm so excited we're finally here in **Greece**!" Violet exclaimed. "We'll get to visit fascinating **archaeological sites**, museums, ancient cities . . ."

"Don't forget, Vi, you promised me some relaxation time on the beach!" Colette said, wagging a paw at her friend.

"Plus, the **FOOD** here is supposed to be amazing," Pam put in.

As if on cue, Kostantina scampered over with a STEAMING serving dish, and the Thea Sisters turned their attention to their first delicious Greek dinner.

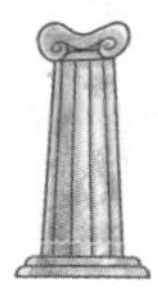

DISCOVERING ATHENS

The next **morning**, the Thea Sisters were up bright and early. They couldn't wait to start exploring the city.

The mouselets were leaving the hotel when Colette realized something. "Uh-oh, I forgot my **sunscreen**! We'll be in the sun all day, so we should be **covered up**."

"Good call, Colette," Paulina said. "Go get it, we'll wait for you **here**."

As they waited, Nicky pulled out a map to show her friends their route for the day. They were all huddled together when they heard shouting: "I don't want anyone to suspect . . ."

There was a rodent **HIDDEN** in the corner of the terrace, arguing on his cell phone. As soon as he noticed the mouselets, he ended his call and turned away.

"That was **weird**," Paulina said.

Just then, Colette rejoined them, with an **ENORMOUSE** bottle in her paw. "Mouselets, I've got my sunscreen! Ready to go?" Then she noticed the distracted expressions on her friends' snouts. *"What's up?"*

"Nothing, just that rodent . . ." But when Paulina turned to point at him, he had **disappeared**.

"All right, let's move those tails! Ancient Athens is waiting," Nicky said. "In a few hours, it'll be **HOTTER** than fondue in a pot."

They began their tour at

the **Acropolis**, the highest part of the city. Many ancient temples, theaters, and monuments had been built there, and some were still standing.

The **mouselets** clambered along the path up the hill. Nicky led the little group, while Violet trailed behind, yawning. "We got up way too early . . ."

But then she spotted the first set of **MARBLE COLUMNS**. "Wow, I think that's the most **fabumouse** thing I've ever seen!"

Paulina opened her **GUIDEBOOK**. "Those are the Propylaea, the columns that mark the entrance to the Acropolis. They were built more than two thousand four hundred years ago."

"And look! That's the Parthenon, right?" Colette asked, indicating a majestic **TEMPLE** that towered over the Acropolis.

Absolutely fabumouse!

"Uh-huh. It's dedicated to the **goddess Athena**, and it's the most important building in the Acropolis," Paulina replied.

"Don't you feel MINUSCULE in front of something this monumental?" Paulina asked.

The others nodded. They were squeakless before such splendor.

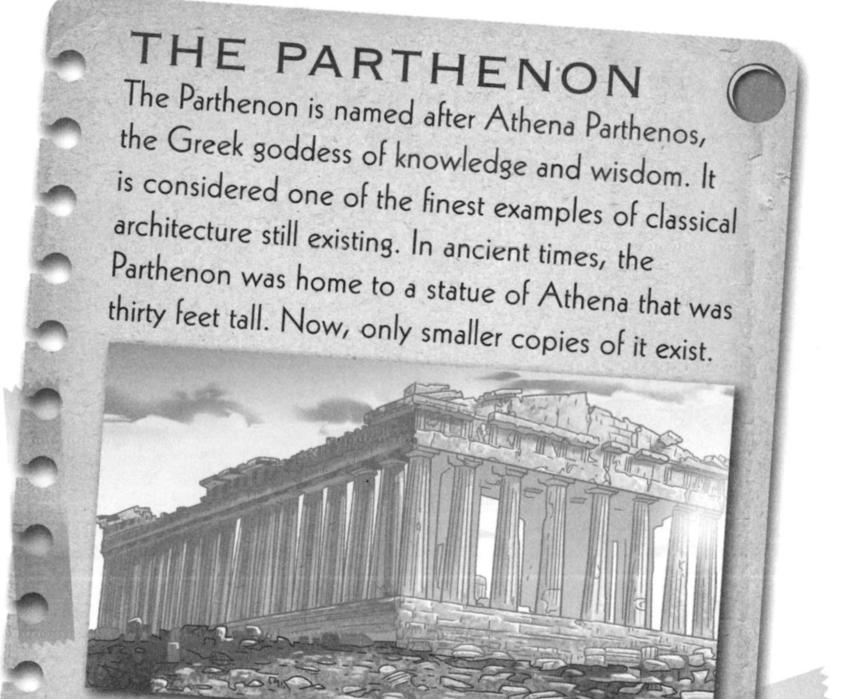

THE PARTHENON

The Parthenon is named after Athena Parthenos, the Greek goddess of knowledge and wisdom. It is considered one of the finest examples of classical architecture still existing. In ancient times, the Parthenon was home to a statue of Athena that was thirty feet tall. Now, only smaller copies of it exist.

A little later, the mouselets reached the **theater** of Dionysus. As they sat down on the stone steps, Violet said, "Did you know the **ancient** Greeks were famouse for writing plays? Isn't it **thrilling** to think some of them were performed right here where we're sitting?"

"Were they LOVE STORIES?" Colette asked.

"No, mostly **tragedies**," Violet replied. "Stories of battles, betrayals, **LONG** journeys . . ."

"Oh," said Colette, wrinkling her snout. "Not a single story with a happy ending?"

Violet laughed, but she didn't want to disappoint her FRIEND. "Let me think about it . . . maybe I'll remember one!"

AN ANCIENT THEATER

The mouselets' two days in **ATHENS** passed in a flash. Soon the **THEA SISTERS** were scurrying out to the terrace to say good-bye to Kostantina.

"It's been a pleasure to have you here. It's a **shame** that you're going so soon . . . but on the other paw, the rest of **Greece** is certainly worth visiting!"

"We've enjoyed it here," said Pam. "But we have to hurry to catch our **bus**!"

The mouselets ran to the station, where they just barely caught the bus to Corinth.

Paulina and Nicky immediately stuck their snouts in their **guidebooks**,

Colette applied a layer of SUNSCREEN, and Pam munched on a cookie Kostantina had packed for her.

As for Violet, she fell into a deep sleep. She woke only when Colette shouted, "Come on, sleepysnout! We have to get off!"

"Huh? Wha?" Violet mumbled. "I was DREAMING. I have to tell you about it . . ."

"You can fill me in later. Let's go!" Colette urged her.

Rubbing her EYES, Violet scrambled off the bus and joined her friends on a large bridge. Below them, a bright blue canal ran between two tall stone walls.

"Smokin' Swiss cheese, where are we?" she cried.

"The CORINTH CANAL, which divides Athens from the Peloponnese, the southernmost part of Greece," Nicky explained.

"It's so gorgeous! I just adore Greece." Colette sighed.

"Wait until you see the ancient THEATER of Epidaurus!" Nicky replied.

"Squeaking of theater . . ." Violet said as they clambered onto the next BUS. "Guess what I was dreaming about? A Greek play that you'd absolutely love, Colette!"

"Really?" her friend replied.

"Yeah! It's a love story, and it has a happy ending. It's called HELEN, and it was written by Euripides," Violet continued.

"*Eupirides?* Who's that?" Pam asked.

"*Euripides!*" Violet corrected her. "One of

THE CORINTH CANAL

This man-made canal was built between 1882 and 1893. It connects the Gulf of Corinth with the Saronic Gulf. It is 3.9 miles long and about 82 feet across at its widest point.

the greatest writers in the ancient world. In *Helen*, he tells the **myth** of a married couple separated by the **TROJAN WAR**. They find each other again after lots of adventures."

Violet **told** her friends the story as their bus drove to Epidaurus. The mouselets had already begun touring the **famouse** theater there by the time she finished her tale.

"How **romantic**!" Colette cried. "Right, Pam? Pam . . . ? Where is she?"

The mouselets were at the **CENTER** of the stage, in the lowest part of the theater.

"I don't see her . . ." Paulina murmured, **squinting**.

"Paaaam!" Colette shouted.

Her squeak **echoed** throughout the theater. In the back row, a rodent was **waving** at her.

"There she is! But how did she hear me?" Colette asked.

"This theater is famouse for its amazing **acoustics**," Violet explained. "You can HEAR the actors from everywhere!"

Pam rejoined her friends. "It's true. I heard every squeak, Coco!"

"**WOW!** Um, what are you eating, Pam?"

"Oh, nothing . . . just an olive sandwich."

HELEN, BY EURIPIDES

The Trojan War has ended, and Menelaus, the king of Sparta, is on his way home with his wife, Helen. But his ship wrecks on the coast of Egypt, and Menelaus discovers that the real Helen is living in the court of the Egyptian king — the one traveling with him is a phantom!

Menelaus is reunited with the real Helen, and they are blissfully happy to be together again. They want to return home, but the Egyptian king wants to marry Helen himself. Helen and Menelaus find a way to escape, and together they set sail for Greece.

"Pam, your belly must be absolutely **bottomless**!" Colette laughed.

Pam nodded. "The stories about my **belly** and its bottomlessness are no myth. But now I'm super thirsty, too."

"Nicky went to get some water," Paulina said. "**THERE** she is!"

Nicky ***RAN*** toward them. "Mouselets, look at this flyer. A **drama festival** is starting here in three days."

"Oh my **GOODMOUSE**! The first play is **Helen**!" said Colette.

"Let's stay here for a few days," Violet said. "We can't miss the **PLAY**!"

A DRAMATIC SCENE

Colette, Nicky, Pam, Paulina, and Violet were looking for a café when they heard a sad squeak. "What a disaster! There's no one as unlucky as me!"

The squeaker was a mouselet pacing back and forth outside the theater like a rodent trapped inside a mousehole. She was squeezing a set of rolled-up papers in one paw.

"Poor thing! I wonder what happened to her," Paulina said.

"My love has abandoned me!" the mouselet exclaimed.

"A broken heart!" Colette said. "Let's see if we can cheer her up."

Colette gently placed a paw on the mouselet's shoulder. "I couldn't HELP overhearing what you said. You mustn't **GIVE UP**!"

The mouselet looked surprised. "What do you mean?"

"Um, well . . ." Colette **faltered**. "I, uh, heard you saying you felt abandoned . . ."

The rodent giggled. "Oh, that's so nice of you! But don't worry, I was just **PRACTICING** my part."

"Your part?" Paulina echoed. "Are you an **actress**?"

"**A great actress!**" a squeak exclaimed.

A tall, **smiling** ratlet was approaching the mouselets. "My name is **Ioannis**, and this is my friend Khloe. We're part of the **theater company** that's performing here."

"Oh, **excuse** me! I'm sorry for intruding . . ." Colette murmured, turning **red**.

Ioannis laughed. "Don't worry. Khloe never misses a chance to practice her part, and when she does, she **FORGETS** about everything around her!"

Violet turned to Khloe. "Now I **UNDERSTAND** — you were rehearsing **HELEN**! That's the part when she's in despair because her husband doesn't recognize her, and she feels all has been lost."

Khloe nodded. "That's right," she said. "But now we have to get back to rehearsal, or we're going to be LATE."

"Yes, we have to get back," Ioannis agreed. "But please come see us on opening night!"

"We'd love to," Colette replied, "but first we need to find a place to stay."

"I can help you," Ioannis said. "My aunt runs an inn nearby. Khloe, the actors, and I are all staying there. Aunt Thalia still has free rooms, and I'm sure she'd be happy to host you."

"That would be great," Violet said. "But we don't want to put you to any trouble . . ."

"It's no trouble!" the ratlet replied. He glanced at Khloe. "We're always happy to make friends with theater lovers like you, right?"

Khloe nodded, but she didn't seem that **interested**.

Ioannis pawed the mouselets a **card** for the Hotel Rhododendron.

"Here, it's not far. And my aunt is a **great cook**!"

Just then, a sharp ***squeak*** interrupted them. "There you are! I need you back onstage pronto!"

"That **grouchy** rodent is our director, Nestor," Ioannis whispered to the Thea Sisters.

"Sorry, Nestor. **We're coming!**" Khloe replied. She scurried away, **DRAGGING** Ioannis along with her.

"Hmm," Paulina said. "I think I've **SEEN** Nestor somewhere before, but I don't remember where . . ."

"Sisters, let's go check out Ioannis's aunt's **hotel**," Pam said. "I know you're going to **tease** me for saying this, but I'm hungrier than a rat in a cheese shop."

"You're not alone, Pam," Violet replied. "I'm starving, too! After all, it's DINNERTIME."

The mouselets scampered toward the EPIDAURUS town center.

IT MUST BE FUN TO BE AN ACTOR

Ioannis was right: Aunt Thalia was a magnificent cook, and her hotel was cheerful and comfortable.

The mouselets chatted until it was late. The next MORNING, when they stumbled sleepily into the breakfast room, they found a surprise on their table: a bouquet of fresh flowers.

"My nephew left those for you," Thalia explained. "And he asked me to give you a message. Now, what was it? Hmm. My memory is lousy these days . . ."

"Maybe he wanted to tell

us **SOMETHING** about the play," Paulina guessed.

"The **PLAY**? Oh yes, of course! He said you could go help with the rehearsal, if you'd like."

"What a **GREAT IDEA**!" said Violet. "Let's go."

A half hour later, the mouselets arrived at the **THEATER**, where the company was busy rehearsing. Nestor stood center stage, giving instructions to an **actor**. Around them were a dozen rodents practicing their lines and adjusting their **COSTUMES**.

"Who are you?" a ratlet in **ancient Greek** clothing asked. "Tourists aren't allowed in here."

"Don't worry, they're friends," said Ioannis,

appearing from behind the set. Khloe was right behind him. "I invited them."

"Oh, well, in that case, allow me to introduce myself: I am Teucer, messenger, friend of Menelaus, son of Telamon!" the ratlet declared with a bow.

"Um, has the cheese slipped off your cracker?" Pam exclaimed, confused.

Ioannis grinned. "You must excuse Nikos — he's a little *too* into his character!"

Everyone burst out LAUGHING.

"How about you, Ioannis? Who are you playing?" Violet asked, curious.

"Menelaus, the king of Sparta . . . and Khloe is my wife, Helen!" he said, taking her paw.

Khloe blushed. Before she could reply, a rodent holding a dress in her paws

This is Nikos!

approached. “Khloe, we still need to choose your costume. Come with me!”

“Of course!” the mouselet replied, hurrying away.

“It must fun to be an **ACTOR**,” Colette commented. “I’ve always *dreamed* of acting, but I’ve never had the opportunity.”

“Oh, I’m sure you’ll get a chance sometime,” said Ioannis. “Hey, why don’t you start by giving me a paw while I practice my lines? I think Khloe will be busy in **wardrobe** for a while.”

“What? Oh . . . I couldn’t . . .”

“Come on, Colette, don’t be shy!” Nicky urged her. “Just pretend you’re in **ancient Greece**!”

REHEARSAL TIME

Colette gathered up her **courage**. She cleared her throat and began. "Look at me. Who knows me better than you do?"

The Thea Sisters sat down to watch. "This is the scene when Menelaus and Helen meet for the first time in a long time, and he doesn't believe that she's really his **wife**," Violet explained in a **LOW** squeak.

"You look like her, it's true . . ." Ioannis recited.

"Do you or do you not believe what you see?" replied Colette, who was becoming more **NATURAL** and **CONFIDENT**.

The pair continued their dialogue and then went on to the next scene, in which Menelaus finally realizes that the real **HELEN** is before him.

"Oh, long-awaited day, when I might take you in my arms again!" cried Ioannis.

"He's really good!" Paulina said softly.

"Yes, and Colette is a total star, too!" Nicky whispered.

"My dear Menelaus, finally, after all this time, I am happy again!" Colette said.

Nicky, Pam, Paulina, and Violet were impressed. They clapped enthusiastically at the scene's end.

Meanwhile, Khloe had returned from her costume fittings, and she was struck DUMB at the sight of Ioannis and Colette rehearsing together.

"Wh-what? Is Ioannis thinking of REPLACING me?!" she sputtered.

"No way! No one could

REPLACE YOU!" said Nikos.

Khloe smiled at her friend. "I wish I were as sure as you are! Ioannis has been acting strange lately . . ."

"What do you mean?" Nikos asked.

Khloe sighed. "He's always distracted, and it seems like he's never paying attention. I've tried talking to him about it, but he says everything's OKAY . . ."

"Well, if he's neglecting you, he's crazier than a cat chasing his own tail," Nikos declared.

Just then, Ioannis and Colette finished their scene, and the THEA SISTERS surrounded Colette, showering her with compliments.

Ioannis saw Khloe and headed toward her, but then his phone rang. "Excuse me . . ." he said, looking at the NUMBER on his phone's screen. He stepped away to take the call.

"You see? Just like I was saying," Khloe told Nikos, shaking her snout. "Lately he's been getting lots of MYSTERIOUS phone calls."

"Yeah, that is weird," said Nikos. "But don't worry about it. You should concentrate on the play! I could help you practice your part." He pawed her a script.

"Thanks, Nikos. You're a good friend," Khloe said.

DANCING THE NIGHT AWAY

After a busy day at the **theater**, the THEA SISTERS returned to Aunt Thalia's inn.

Thalia had been busy, too. She and her husband, Kosmas, had MOVED all the tables on the terrace against the walls, creating a big open space in the middle. And Thalia had prepared a TRADITIONAL DINNER for the mouselets and the theater company. After dinner, there would be a dance performance.

The Thea Sisters took a quick ratnap, and then joined the PARTY. The only one missing was Colette, who tried on every outfit in her SUITCASE before she came down.

"Colette, thank goodmouse you MADE IT! A

few more minutes and Pam would have eaten everything," Nicky joked.

Pam rolled her eyes. "Hey, I'm just paying the proper respect to Aunt Thalia's home-grown goodies!"

The ACTORS from the theater company were all there, including Khloe and Nikos, who were chatting in a corner. Only Ioannis was missing.

"Where's your REHEARSAL partner, Colette?" Paulina asked.

"You mean me?" came a squeak from BEHIND them.

"Ioannis! What's that? A costume from the play?" asked Pam in surprise.

The ratlet laughed. He was wearing white pants, a billowy shirt with a red belt, a colorful vest, and shoes with pom-poms on them.

"It's my outfit for the **sirtaki**," he replied.

"For what?"

"The sirtaki, a GREEK dance. You'll see!"

A moment later, lively music filled the room, at first slow and then becoming faster and faster.

The hotel's **GUESTS** formed a line, with Ioannis in the middle, and started to dance together in small, graceful jumps.

The mouselets started to **clap** their paws in time. They watched for a few moments, till they'd learned the steps, and then joined the dance.

"Follow me!" Ioannis urged them.

The terrace was filled with the thunder of pawsteps as the

Costume for the sirtaki

La la la!
La la la!

La la la!
La la la!

dancers whirled and **twirled**.

Khloe joined the dance, too, as Ioannis's partner.

The evening passed in a *FLASH*. Just before midnight, the Thea Sisters decided to turn in for the night. Their paws were aching from all that dancing!

Tired but happy, the mouselets stopped to admire the STARRY sky reflected in the ocean. Then they headed up to their ROOMS and went straight to sleep.

A PERFECT DAY TO RELAX!

The next morning, the mouselets woke up with the melody of the **sirtaki** still ringing in their ears.

"What's the plan for **TODAY**, Sisters?" Pam asked at breakfast.

"We could go to Mycenae, to visit the **archaeological site**," Violet began.

"Or we could rent bicycles and visit the countryside," Nicky suggested. "I saw a bicycle path on the **map**. It's long, but it goes through a really beautiful area, and —"

"Now, wait just one minute, mouselings!" Colette exclaimed. "Are we on vacation or what?"

"Yes, but —" Violet replied.

"No buts! Vacation means at least a few days of perfect **relaxation** on the **beach**. Otherwise, why did I fill my suitcase with bathing suits and sundresses?!"

Violet laughed. "You have a point, Coco! Okay, the beach it is."

Colette pulled a large **PINK BAG** out from under the table. It was filled with bottles of sunscreen, a sun hat, **SUNGLASSES**, towels, and even an inflatable raft.

"Something tells me that Colette has our day all planned out," said Nicky, **WINKING**.

"You bet! Thalia and Kosmas **RECOMMENDED** a spot not far from here," Colette explained. "What do you say, are we ready to go?"

Less than a half hour later, the mouselets were STRETCHED OUT on a marvemouse beach.

Nicky started blowing up an inflatable raft. "Who's coming with me for a DIP?"

Colette opened one eye. "I just started working on my tan! I'll join you in a little while . . ."

Pam sprang toward Nicky, grabbed the RAFT, and jumped into the water, shouting, "Come on, Sisters! Last one in is a rotten cheese puff!"

The others leaped after their friend. Even Colette jumped to her paws. "Wait, I don't want to be the LAST one in!"

The mouselets stayed in the crystal blue water for a long time, splashing, PLAYING, and swimming.

Wait for me!
Try and catch me!
We're coming!

After a few hours, they decided they'd had enough sun, so they started walking back to the **inn**.

"I wonder if Ioannis has finished learning his lines," Violet said as they scampered along.

The mouselets exchanged **GLANCES**. Finally, Colette said what everyone was thinking. "Why don't we **stop by** and see how rehearsals are going?"

At the theater, the **THEA SISTERS** discovered that yesterday's cheerful atmosphere had disappeared like cheddar in a cheese grater. The **actors** were pacing nervously back and forth, and Nestor held his snout in his paws. His whiskers were quivering with **worry**.

"What happened?" Paulina asked Ioannis, who came over to greet them.

"It's a total **CAT-ASTROPHE**," the ratlet sighed. "The mouselet playing the guardian of the **king's palace** fell down . . ."

"Oh, no! Is she **HURT**?"

"Nothing serious — Melina just sprained her ankle. But she won't be able to perform on **opening** night. We might have to postpone the **PLAY**!"

We might have to postpone the play!

A DREAM COME TRUE

"There's no **UNDERSTUDY**?" Violet asked Ioannis.

"Unfortunately, no, we don't have any available **actresses**, and —"

Before Ioannis could finish, Nestor POINTED his paw at Colette. "You! You!"

"Me?" said Colette, turning to see if Nestor was pointing at someone behind her. "Um, what about me?"

"**You are the answer!** I heard you reading some lines yesterday. You are **expressive**. With a little practice, you could stand in for Melina."

"But I . . ." Colette faltered, **BLUSHING**. "I can't suddenly become an actress!"

Me?!

Yes, you!

"I'll help you," Ioannis said.

"Perfect. Then it's **decided**," Nestor concluded. "Come on, break's over, back to work! I want you in your places in three minutes!" he **SHOUTED** to the other actors.

"What a bossy rodent," Violet whispered.

"Maybe so, but he's right. Colette is the only one who can **HELP US**!" Ioannis replied. "Come on, let's go work on your **PART**."

Khloe stepped forward. "But, Ioannis, you have to rehearse with me . . ."

"You're already **WONDERFUL**, Khloe!" the ratlet reassured her. "It's better if I help Colette."

Khloe scurried away without another word. Violet noticed that her eyes were shining with tears. Ioannis was so busy helping Colette, he didn't notice a thing.

"Poor Khloe," Violet said.

"But Ioannis is right. Khloe is already a grcat ACTRESS. And she already knows her part, while Colette has to learn everything," Pam replied.

"That's true, but still . . ." said Violet, "I think he hurt Khloe's FEELINGS."

Little by little, Colette began to learn Melina's part. She was playing the old guardian Menelaus meets at the door of the palace where the real HELEN lives.

"Who goes there? Get out of here don't stop here . . ." she RECITED.

"Hey, stop and breathe! Otherwise the audience won't understand a word," said

Ioannis, giving her a kind **SMILE**.

"You're right," Colette said. "I'm just a little nervous . . ."

"Don't WORRY. Just put yourself in the character's shoes and forget everything else."

"Is that what you do?" Colette asked.

"Yes, when I'm acting I forget the real world," said Ioannis. "**Let's try it** together! Now you are an ancient rodent, and I am **Menelaus** . . ."

Colette took a deep **breath**. *"Who goes there? Get out of here, don't stop here!"*

"You could say it more kindly!" Ioannis replied, **ANNOYED**.

Colette blushed. "I'm sorry, I was just trying to lose myself in the part . . ."

Ioannis burst out **laughing**. "No, no, that's my linc! You're doing great!"

Encouraged, Colette continued reciting her lines as her friends **WATCHED** from the wings.

"Colette is going to be **GREAT**," Paulina commented.

"I think so, too. Right now, I think she'll have the biggest problem with her wardrobe!" Violet giggled, pointing to a huge white **wig**.

Pam grinned. "Our stylish Coco is absolutely going to love that!"

A SUDDEN DISAPPEARANCE

The next two **days** passed in a flash. Colette was practicing her part **AROUND THE CLOCK**.

"At least tomorrow is *opening night*,"

Paulina said as they sat down at the breakfast table. "If I have to hear that scene one more time, I'm going to lose my cheese!"

"Come on, mouselets, move those paws! I'm going be late for rehearsal," exclaimed Colette. She was clutching her script. "Today Ioannis is going to show me a few tricks for dealing with STAGE FRIGHT!"

But there was no trace of Ioannis at the theater, and none of the actors knew where he was.

"That's weird," said Violet, frowning.

"Where could he be?" Colette wondered.

She saw Khloe and scampered over. "Hi, Khloe, have you SEEN Ioannis today?"

"No," Khloe replied. "I assumed he was helping you with your part, as usual."

Just then, Charissa, the **costume assistant**, joined them. "Mouselets, have you seen Ioannis? I've been **LOOKING** for him for hours! We were supposed to have a fitting at eight a.m."

"We're trying to find him, too," Violet explained. "We don't know **where** he is."

"Something smells stinkier than putrid feta," Colette said. "Ioannis is always ON TIME!"

"Maybe Nestor can help," Nicky suggested. "There he is. Let's ask him."

The show's director looked even more ANXIOUS than usual. He scurried toward the mouselets sighing and shaking his snout. He held a SHEET of paper tight in his paws.

"I don't believe this! Ioannis is playing tricks on me!" he shouted at Khloe.

Khloe looked more surprised than a kitten in a dog kennel. Nestor **stuck** the paper in her snout. "Check this out!"

Khloe began to ***read aloud***.

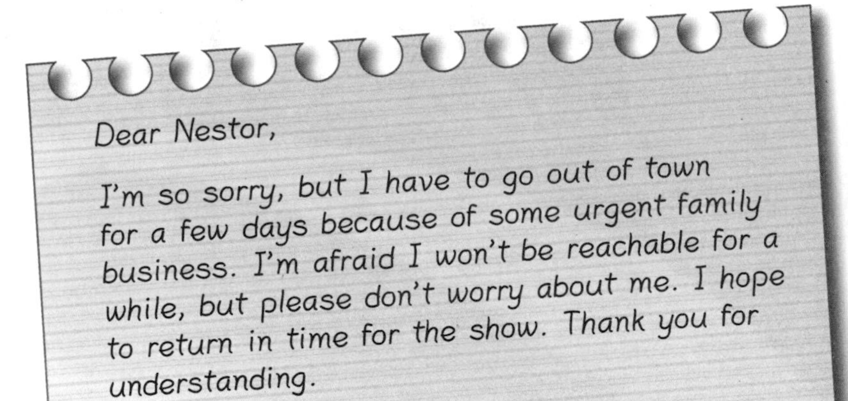

Dear Nestor,

I'm so sorry, but I have to go out of town for a few days because of some urgent family business. I'm afraid I won't be reachable for a while, but please don't worry about me. I hope to return in time for the show. Thank you for understanding.

See you soon,
Ioannis

The mouselet let the **PAPER** slip from her paws. "I can't believe he left without telling me . . ." she gasped.

At that MOMENT, Nikos joined the group. "What's going on?" he asked.

"Ioannis had to **Leave** because of family business," Violet explained.

"Cheese sticks! His business is to stay here and perform," Nestor cried. "Tomorrow is opening night! I need a missing actor like **mold** on a fresh slice of mozzarella. If Ioannis thinks he can scamper off and then show up at the last **MINUTE**, he's got another thing coming!"

"This is terrible for the show!" cried Nikos, shaking his snout.

"Khloe, do you know what happened?"

But the mouselet had already run off with tears in her **EYES**.

Colette looked thoughtful. "Something **VERY SERIOUS** must have happened," she murmured. "I can't believe Ioannis would just leave without squeaking to anyone."

"**Crusty carburetors**, I don't like this story one bit!" Pam exclaimed.

"You'll see, he'll **come back**," Paulina said, trying to lift her friends' spirits. "Tomorrow is an **IMPORTANT** day for him."

"I hope you're right . . ." Colette **whispered**.

DO YOU TRUST US?

Nikos tried to catch up with Khloe. "Hey, **WAIT FOR ME**!" he called.

The mouselet turned, but kept her snout down. "What is it?"

"I wanted to tell you — don't worry about Ioannis. **I'M SURE HE'S FINE . . .**"

"Of course he's fine! He left without telling me anything," Khloe cried. "He didn't stop to **think** about me for a second."

"Don't get your tail in a twist, Khloe," Nikos said kindly. "Forget about him and concentrate on the **play**."

"I don't feel like rehearsing now. I'm going

to take a walk," Khloe replied.

"Do you want me to come with you?" Nikos asked.

The mouselet **shook** her snout. "Thanks, but I'd like to be alone for a bit."

Meanwhile, the other actors were rehearsing their scenes. Colette had to get back to work, too, on Nestor's **orders**.

"Sprained ankles, disappearing actors . . . what's next?!" muttered the director, **PACING** back and forth like a cat outside a mousehole.

"Sisters, I know what we need to perk us up — a nice **snack**!" Pam suggested.

"Good idea," **Violet** said. "I'm more ravenous than a rodent on a MouseFast diet. I saw a snack cart outside. I'll go pick up a few things."

The moment Violet set paw outside the theater, she heard a muffled sob. She followed the sound to a bench where Khloe sat alone. Violet **CLEARED** her throat.

The actress lifted her tear-stained snout and saw her. "Oh . . . I'd like to be alone, please."

Violet was very wise for such a young mouselet. She knew that sometimes a rodent's snout says one thing, but her **heart** wants something else. At that moment, Khloe needed a friend. So Violet sat down, offered her a tissue, and waited for Khloe to squeak.

Khloe sniffled for another minute. "I don't **UNDERSTAND**," she said at last. "Until just a few weeks ago, Ioannis and I were best friends. But lately he's started to act funny, like he's keeping a

SECRET from me. And now he's gone!"

"Do you know what his family trouble is?" Violet asked.

Khloe shook her snout. "I'm not sure. But it might just be an excuse to **get away** . . ."

"I'm sure there's an explanation," Violet said kindly. "I don't know

Ioannis well, but he seems like an **HONEST** ratlet."

"He used to be," Khloe replied sadly. "But lately he hasn't been telling the whole truth. I have so many **QUESTIONS** . . ."

"Why don't you let me help? We'll find answers to your questions **together**," Violet said.

"Together?"

"Of course! You, me, and the other Thea Sisters," said Violet, **smiling**. "Do you trust us?"

For a moment, it was so quiet, you could hear a cheese slice drop. Violet could see Khloe was torn. But eventually, the other mouselet decided to **trust** her.

"All right," Khloe said, taking Violet's outstretched paw. "Let's go find your friends."

NO LUCK

Pam WAVED to Violet. "Hey! Where's our snack? I'm starving!"

"Pam, I'm afraid your stomach will have to wait," her friend replied.

"Sorry! It's my fault. I distracted her," Khloe explained with a shy **smile**.

Just then, Colette scurried over. She was in full costume. "Mouselets, hide me from Nestor! I need a minute to catch my breath!"

"That mouse is BOSSIER than a beaver building a dam," Khloe **joked**.

"Oh, Khloe, there you are! We've been looking for you," Colette said.

"I needed to CLEAR my head. But after squeaking with Violet, I decided to ask you all for **help**," Khloe said.

"Sizzling spark plugs, of course we'll help you!" Pam said. "Um . . . help with what?"

"Help her figure out **WHERE** Ioannis is," Violet explained.

Colette nodded. "Great idea. We've got to stick together. Friends together, mice forever!"

"You!" a squeak boomed. "There you are! Get onstage and keep on **practicing**! Khloe — you, too!"

The two mouselets had no choice but to follow Nestor's **ORDERS**. As they scurried away, Khloe WHISPERED, "Go see Aunt Thalia. Maybe she knows something."

The mouselets decided to follow Khloe's advice. They scampered back toward the **inn** as fast as their paws could take them.

When they arrived, **Aunt Thalia** was busy cleaning the entryway.

"Um, excuse me . . ." Paulina said.

"Oh, hi there! You're back already?" asked Aunt Thalia. "Would you like me to make you a **SNACK**?"

Pam was about to say yes, but Nicky didn't give her a chance. "No, thank you. We're actually here to ask you about Ioannis."

"Isn't he a darling ratlet? Ever since he was a mouseling he's loved acting! He's won many awards! See this?" Aunt Thalia said, pointing at a TROPHY. "He won it when he was only seven!"

"He's very talented," Paulina agreed. "Um, we were wondering if Ioannis said anything unusual to you **LAST NIGHT**."

Aunt Thalia reflected for a moment. "Oh, yes, he did! He wanted me to prepare

My darling nephew!

*moussaka** tonight for your dinner," she **REPLIED**. "That's my specialty, you know."

"So he didn't say anything about any trouble?" asked Pam.

"**TROUBLE?** No, nothing like that," Aunt Thalia replied. "Why, should I be worried?"

"Oh, no, of course not!" said Pam quickly. "We just want to, um, **surprise** him on his opening night."

Nicky thanked Aunt Thalia, and the **THEA SISTERS** moved out to the courtyard.

"Mouselets, we've run out of clues. I don't know what to do next," said Violet.

Paulina nodded. "All we can do is wait for Ioannis to show up in the **fur**!"

* *Moussaka* is a traditional Greek dish: an eggplant and meat pie.

SOMETHING'S NOT RIGHT

That **night**, none of the Thea Sisters slept well. They were all thinking of their new friend and his mysterious **DISAPPEARANCE**. They tossed and turned like kittens with a new ball of yarn.

The next morning, the mouselets rolled out of bed early, hoping that Ioannis had returned or that there would be **news** from him. Unfortunately, there was nothing, so they decided to dedicate the **day** to their search. They would begin by exploring the area around **EPIDAURUS**. Maybe someone had seen Ioannis before he left.

Colette, Nicky, Pamela, Paulina, and Violet ate a **quick** breakfast and scurried out of the inn.

When they'd gone a few steps, they heard Aunt Thalia calling after them. "Mouselets, just a minute! I found a **NOTE** Ioannis left for you yesterday. I put it in my apron pocket and then **FORGOT** all about it! I am so sorry."

"No worries," Pam said. She took the note and **read** it aloud to her friends.

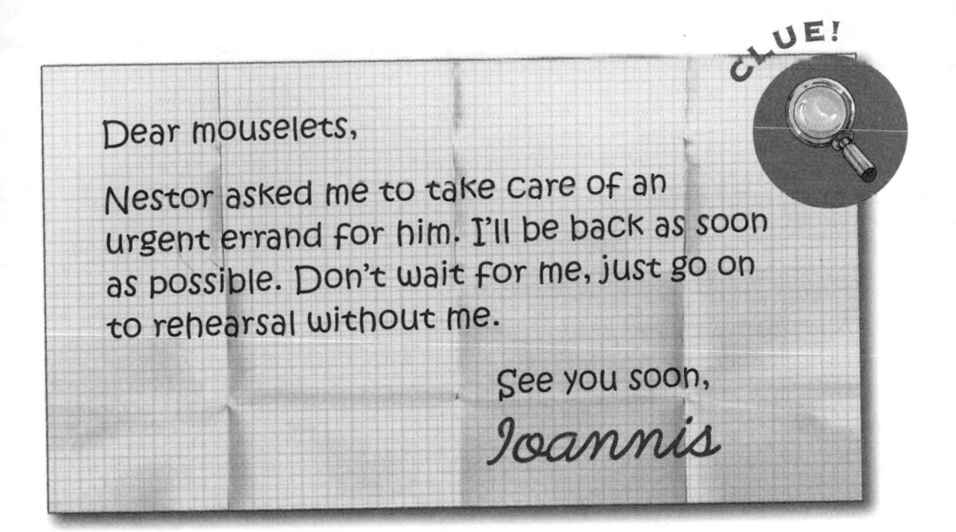

"That's why he left!" Paulina cried.

"But in the note he left with Nestor, Ioannis talked about a family emergency," Nicky said.

"Mumbling mufflers, I don't understand this at all," Pam said.

"There's only one rodent who can clear this up," Violet said. "Nestor!"

Suddenly, Paulina's eyes lit up. "Now I remember where I've seen Nestor before! He was the mysterious rodent on the phone at our hotel in Athens!"

Ioannis left two different notes, with two different reasons for his absence. Why? Could one note be a fake?

"I knew it! That mouse has always seemed kind of shady," Pam said.

"Shady, and a little **HARSH**," Colette put in. Over the last few days, Nestor hadn't missed a chance to **criticize** her performance.

"Well, what are we waiting for?" Nicky said. "There's no point standing around here with our tails in a twist. Let's go ask him to **explain** himself!"

ON NESTOR'S TAIL

As soon as they reached the **THEATER**, the mouselets started looking for Nestor.

"You're here awfully early," said Khloe in surprise.

Violet nodded. "Yes, we found a clue back at the inn."

"It's a **note** Ioannis left for us," Paulina explained. "Check it out."

Khloe **twisted** her whiskers as she scanned the paper. "Wait . . . what? This doesn't match the **message** Ioannis left for Nestor!"

"Exactly," Pam said. "We came to **find** Nestor to ask him about it."

"Nestor just **LEFT**," Khloe said.

"We've got to catch up with him!" Nicky exclaimed.

"Okay, let's go!" Khloe replied.

Violet shook her snout. "You and Colette should stay here. You need to rehearse. Plus, we need you here in case **Ioannis** returns or gets in touch."

"All right," Khloe responded **reluctantly**. "Keep me posted, okay?"

Nicky, Violet, Paulina, and Pam scurried off in the direction Khloe had indicated. After a few minutes, they **ended up** at the bus station.

"LOOK over there!" said Nicky. Nestor was climbing onto a bus. The doors closed behind him, and the bus zoomed away.

"We missed him by a WHISKER!" Violet panted. "Now what?"

"Relax, Sisters!" exclaimed Pam, smiling. "I got a look at its destination: MYCENAE!*"

"There's another bus to Mycenae leaving soon," Paulina said.

The mouselets ran to the ticket window. There was only one rodent ahead of them.

"We have five minutes before the next bus leaves," Violet said, checking her watch.

But the rodent ahead of them was very demanding. "I need to go to Athens," he told the ticket mouse.

"One TICKET, right away," she replied.

"The bus has air conditioning, right?"

"Yes."

"But not too cold, okay? And PLEASE get me a good seat! Not in the front, but not in the back . . ."

"So, in the middle?" suggested Violet impatiently.

* Mycenae is a famous Greek archaeological site. To see where it's located, check the map on page 11.

"Okay, the middle!" the rodent agreed.

The mouselets were **SEETHING** with impatience. Finally, it was their turn.

"Four tickets for Mycenae, please!" Nicky rattled off. Then she and the other mouselets dashed for the bus.

"**PUFF . . . PANT . . .** I feel like an out-of-shape gerbil on a brand-new wheel. This vacation is turning out to be **WAY** less relaxing than I expected!" gasped Pam.

SHEEP CROSSING!

As the bus zipped along, the THEA SISTERS tried to figure out how to keep tabs on **Nestor**.

"I wonder how big Mycenae is," Nicky said.

Paulina pulled out her **MousePhone** to check, when . . .

SCREEEEEEEEEEEEEECHHHHHH!

The driver slammed on the brakes. They were stuck right behind another **BUS**!

Nicky **LEANED** out the window to see what was happening. "The bus in front of us stopped to let a flock of SHEEP go by."

"That's **Nestor's** bus! It must have been stuck here for a while," Colette said.

"Sisters, this is our LUCKY DAY," Pam declared. "We've already caught up with him!"

A moment later, the two buses started up again. They arrived in MYCENAE at the same time.

The THEA SISTERS began following **Nestor** through the streets of Mycenae. He immediately started walking toward the **archaeological site**.

"Maybe Nestor wants to learn more about

MYCENAE

Mycenae is an ancient city located not far from Epidaurus. It was home to the legendary king Agamemnon, who commanded the Greek armies during the Trojan War. The German archaeologist Heinrich Schliemann, who is considered the modern discoverer of ancient Greece, began excavating the city in the 1860s.

In Mycenae, Schliemann discovered the famous Mask of Agamemnon, a golden funeral mask thought to have been made for King Agamemnon. After many years of study, scholars have agreed that the mask actually predates the famous king.

ancient Mycenean civilization," Nicky guessed, checking her GUIDEBOOK. "There was an ancient city here. Archaeologists didn't discover it until the 1860s."

"Mouselets, look!" said Paulina, pointing to a gateway made of STONE.

"It's the LION GATE!" Nicky explained. "It was built around 1300 CE, and —"

"Tell us later, Nic. Nestor just stopped!" Pam hissed.

"He's waiting for someone," Paulina whispered. "Let's blend in with those TOURISTS so we can keep an eye on him."

A few minutes later, a rodent wearing big, round sunglasses approached Nestor.

The two mice shook paws and started talking. The only one close enough to hear them was Violet.

"Sorry we had to meet here," the rodent

GAME
Can you find Violet, Nicky, Paulina, and Pam?
Answer: Pam and Violet are on the left side of the
page, and Nicky and Paulina are on the right!

told Nestor. "I was hoping for a quiet place to **TALK**."

Nestor looked **ANNOYED**. "But, Michael, this place is packed with rodents! Someone could hear us and discover our secret . . ."

Violet took a step closer. *What could the secret be?*

"Well, there's no need to keep it a secret any longer. You can make the **announcement**!"

"So it's true? Our tour of the **BEST** theaters in Europe is on?!" Nestor asked. "I can't wait to tell the actors the **GOOD NEWS**!"

Violet couldn't help herself. "A **TOUR**?!" she gasped.

The two rodents turned toward her in **shock**.

"Hey, what are you doing here?!" Nestor cried.

FALSE TRAILS AND HIDDEN CLUES

Nicky, Pam, and Paulina **rushed** over to Violet.

"What's going on, Vi?" Nicky asked.

"Oh, nothing," Violet said. "Our **suspicions** were all wrong—"

"Suspicions?" Nestor interrupted. "What in the name of string cheese are you talking about?"

Paulina took a deep breath. "Something about Ioannis's **disappearance** didn't seem right to us," she explained. "You showed us a note that mentioned family business, but Aunt Thalia **passed on** a different message from Ioannis." She pawed Nestor the **note** that Ioannis had left at the inn.

Nestor **SCANNED** it. "Errand? I didn't ask him to take care of an **errand**!" he sputtered.

"We thought you had something to do with Ioannis's disappearance," Violet said. "We heard you **scheming** with someone on the phone in Athens. Then today, when we **saw**

you leave in such a hurry, we thought . . ."

". . . that I was hiding the **TRUTH** about Ioannis?" Nestor said, laughing. "I'm afraid your theory has more holes than a slice of Swiss, mouselets. I came to Mycenae for a business matter, the same reason I went to **Athens** a few days ago! This is Michael Rattis, a producer who's just arranged a **European tour** for our production of *Helen*."

"**Cheese niblets!** Why would Ioannis leave a fake message with Aunt Thalia?" Pam sighed.

Michael took a step forward. "Mouselets, you seem **so sincere** about finding your friend. Nestor and I would love to give you a paw. I love a good mystery! Tell us what you know, and maybe we can help you figure it out."

Violet glanced over at her friends. They nodded. So she **told** Nestor and Michael everything.

Michael remained silent for a few moments, scratching his snout. "We have two **notes** saying different things. One must be from Ioannis, because he gave it to his aunt personally, but it talks about an errand that doesn't exist. And Nestor's note mentions a **family** emergency . . ."

HERE'S THE SITUATION:

- Nestor found a message from Ioannis saying he needed to go away because of urgent family business.
- Ioannis left a note with his aunt saying that he was away on an errand for Nestor.
- One of the two notes must be a fake, but which one?
- Nestor said he didn't give Ioannis an errand to run. Is he lying? Or was Ioannis tricked?

"But why would Ioannis have written two different reasons?" wondered Violet.

"Good question. We can deduce that **Nestor's** letter is probably fake. Maybe someone asked your friend to do an errand and **PRETENDED** it was for Nestor!"

"**Wavering whiskers!**" Pam exclaimed. "But if Ioannis has been tricked, he could be in **DANGER**!"

"And he certainly won't get back in time for opening night," Nestor groaned. "I need to find an **understudy** so we don't have to cancel the show!"

"And we need to think about how to find Ioannis," Colette said. "But where do we even **START**?"

There was a moment of silence. Then Paulina squeaked up. "We can't give up, mouselets! The key to solving a **MYSTERY** is paying attention to the details. We might already have the clues we need to find Ioannis, we just need to **LOOK** at them in the right away!"

A CLUE REVIEW!

The THEA SISTERS and Nestor began their trip back to Epidaurus.

The director had one thing on his mind: how to replace his lead ACTOR. "We're just a few hours from opening night! Who could possibly play Menelaus?" he groaned, clenching his **PAWS**. "If I find out who did this . . ."

As for the mouselets, they were focused on how to find their friend, and whether he might be in trouble.

"We need to tell Khloe everything," Nicky said. "She may know something **important**, even if she doesn't realize it."

"Yes, the clues we have aren't getting us anywhere," Violet added. She glanced at Ioannis's **note** in her paws. "Details . . . just need to **LOOK** at them the right way . . ." she murmured. "Of course! That's it! Anyone have a **PENCIL**?"

Paulina passed her one. Violet began to **shade** one corner of the paper with the pencil. "There's something hidden here!"

Dear mouselets,

Nestor asked me to take care of an urgent errand for him. I'll be back as soon as possible. Don't wait for me, just go on to rehearsal without me.

See you soon,
Ioannis

BIG BLUE

"You're right! Mouselets, look!" Paulina said.

The words "**BIG BLUE**" had appeared on the paper.

"Before he wrote **this note**, Ioannis wrote 'Big Blue' on the sheet of paper above this one. Then he tore off that sheet and took it with him, but the **impression** remains," Violet explained.

"This is the most important **CLUE** we've found so far," Paulina said.

"But what does '**BIG BLUE**' mean?" asked Pam.

The mouselets and Nestor exchanged a confused **LOOK**: They had no idea!

A USELESS CLUE?

As soon as she saw the Thea Sisters enter the **theater**, Khloe scurried offstage to meet them. "Hi! What did you find out?"

Nestor **APPEARED** behind the mouselets. "They found out that I have nothing to do with your **FRIEND'S** disappearance!"

"But . . . wh-what . . ." Khloe stuttered as Nestor ***stalked*** off, muttering to himself.

Violet placed a paw on Khloe's shoulder. "It's true, Nestor had nothing to do with it. It looks like someone **PROBABLY** tricked Ioannis into leaving Epidaurus."

"So ***where*** is he now?" Khloe asked.

"We don't know, but we did find a new clue. Before he disappeared, Ioannis wrote down the words '**BIG BLUE**'. Do you know what that means?"

"Big Blue is the name of his favorite rock band. He wanted to buy tickets for their next concert," Khloe replied.

"Hmm . . . I DON'T KNOW how that could be related," Paulina murmured.

Colette and Nikos scampered over and joined their group.

"Mouselets, what **SAD** snouts! What happened? No news about Ioannis?" Nikos asked.

"The only **CLUE** we have is the phrase 'Big Blue,'" Khloe replied.

Nikos was startled. "What?"

"Yeah, that's his favorite rock band. Nothing useful for our investigation," Paulina explained.

A discouraged silence fell over the young rodents.

"Khloe, didn't you say that Ioannis has been getting **strange** phone calls lately?" Nikos asked.

"Yes," the mouselet said, looking down in the snout. "He was definitely hiding **something** from me . . ."

"If that's the case, the reason he left probably has something to do with his secret," Nikos concluded. "All we can do is wait for him to RETURN."

"No, we can't," Pam protested. "He could be in danger!"

"**What makes you think that?** He just left yesterday. I'm sure he'll turn up soon," the ratlet replied.

At Nikos's words, the **COLOR** returned to Khloe's snout. "Maybe you're right."

"But, Khloe, that doesn't seem likely," Paulina said. "Ioannis wouldn't —"

He's hiding
something from me!

"Nikos! I'm looking for you! Come here!" Nestor thundered from the wings.

"Sorry, Nestor, I was just taking a little break," the ratlet said. "I'll get back to practicing my part."

"Forget that part! We'll find a substitute. From now on, you'll play the role of Menelaus!"

The mouselets' jaws FELL OPEN like a pack of hungry cats at feeding time.

"What?!" Nikos asked.

"We're running out of time, and I can't WAIT for Ioannis to return," Nestor explained. "You're the only one who can replace him, Nikos."

"But I . . . I don't know if . . ." the ratlet spluttered.

"Nestor's right," Khloe said, nodding. "You're the only one who knows the role."

"Come on, move those paws! We've got to rehearse your new scenes," Nestor **ordered**.

Khloe arranged to meet up with the mouselets later. Then she scurried after Nikos.

"Do you think that Nikos could be right? Did Ioannis go away for some secret reason?" asked Nicky **uncertainly**.

Paulina **shook** her snout confidently. "I think there's something else going on. And we won't give up until we **find out** what."

A DELICIOUS DISCOVERY

"Curdled cream cheese, I just don't get it." Pam sighed. She and the other Thea Sisters were sitting around a big table at an ice cream shop.

They had left Colette at the theater for dress rehearsal while they followed up on a few more clues. But everything was a dead end. The mouselets were **stuck** like flies in fondue. So they'd decided to stop for a snack.

"This ratlet is harder to find than a cheese slice in a haystack. We've looked everywhere, but no one's **SEEN** him," Paulina said.

"I'll bet a little *brain food* will spark some new ideas," Pam said. She grabbed the

Have you seen this ratlet?
No, sorry!
Have you seen this ratlet?
Uh-uh, he hasn't come by here!
Have you seen this ratlet?
No, not recently.

menu. "Hey, there's an ice-cream sundae called **BIG BLUE**!"

"Maybe Ioannis wanted to come here for ice cream," Nicky said.

"Holey cheese, and here we were thinking it might be an important clue." Violet moaned.

"Well, I'm going to try it," Pam said. "It might not lead us to **Ioannis**, but at least it'll fill my hungry belly!"

When the waiter brought their orders, everyone stared at Pam's sundae.

"Pam, your ice cream is strawberry and vanilla — **red** and WHITE! So why is it called 'Big Blue'?" asked Paulina.

"'**BIG BLUE**' is the nickname of an abandoned lighthouse down the coast," their waiter explained. "This sundae named after it is one of our SPECIALTIES."

It looks like
a lighthouse!

Maybe Big Blue was the **CLUE** the mouselets were looking for after all!

"Do you know how to find this **lighthouse**?" Violet asked the waiter.

"Sorry, I'm not from Epidaurus. I'm just working here for the **summer**."

"No worries," Violet said, paying for their **ice cream**.

Paulina, Nicky, and Violet got to their paws. Only Pam remained seated. "Hey, **SISTERS**, we're not going to abandon my Big Blue, are we?"

"Come on, Pam, we can't lose this **CHANCE** to shine a light on the mystery of Ioannis's disappearance!" replied Nicky.

Pam managed to **taste** the very top of her lighthouse sundae. Then she followed the others toward the town **CENTER**.

Big Blue is a lighthouse. But what does it have to do with Ioannis's disappearance?

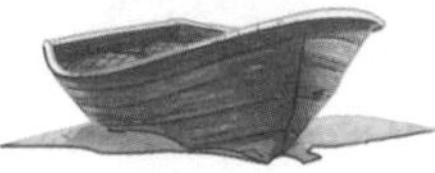

THE FISHERMICE

The THEA SISTERS were back on Ioannis's trail, this time with a concrete clue to investigate.

Unfortunately, all the stores in town were closed for the afternoon, and the HEAT kept everyone inside their houses. The streets were DESERTED!

"This town is emptier than a candy store the day after Halloween! And we're so close to solving the mystery . . ." Violet groaned.

"We hope we're close," Paulina muttered. "It's only a few hours until opening night! If this turns out to be another RED HERRING, we're in trouble."

"Snouts up, mouselets," Nicky exclaimed. "I think we're on the right track. We're going to find Big Blue, I can feel it in my whiskers! Are you with me?"

Violet, Pam, and Paulina NODDED.

"Let's try to think this through. What does a lighthouse do?" Violet asked.

"It guides sailors," Pam replied. "But this is an old lighthouse . . ."

"Then we must ask some old sailors!" Nicky suggested. "Hey, squeaking of herrings, how about those fishermice over there?" She scurried toward them without waiting for an answer.

Violet squinted in the direction Nicky had headed. "Wait, isn't that Aunt Thalia's husband? Kosmas?"

Big Blue?

"It sure is!" Paulina said. "Let's ask him!"

Violet, Pam, and Paulina hurried after Nicky. She was already squeaking with Kosmas and several other fishermice repairing their nets on the dock.

By the time they reached her, Nicky was smiling with satisfaction. "They know where Big Blue is!"

"Of course we know! That old lighthouse has guided sailors across the big blue sea for years. There are lots of MYTHS about that place, you know," a sailor with a sunbeaten snout said.

"What kind of myths?" Pam asked.

"Oh, that it's HAUNTED by ghosts. You know, stuff like that," another fishermouse added, chuckling.

"If you want to visit Big Blue, you'll need to scurry over," the first rodent continued.

"It takes a few hours to get there."

The mouselets shared a discouraged look. They didn't have much **time**!

"We could RENT bikes," Nicky suggested. "We'd get there ***FASTER*** than on paw!"

"I'll give you a lift, mouselets," Kosmas said, looking up from his nets for the first time. "Any friends of my nephew's are friends of mine!"

The mouselets didn't want to tell Kosmas they were actually looking for his nephew. But they were glad to have his **help**!

THE MYSTERIOUS BIG BLUE

The Thea Sisters squeezed into Kosmas's van, which started up with a deep **rumble**. Soon they were zipping down a **ROAD** that hugged the coast.

"Look at that view!" Nicky cried, pointing to the bright blue sea.

"It's **breathtaking**! Right, Vi?" Pam asked her friend. "Violet?"

Violet's snout was greener than mold on aged cheddar.

"**UH-OH**," Paulina said. "It's this twisty road. I'm afraid Violet's going to toss her cheese . . ."

After a few more sharp turns, Kosmas announced, "We're getting close. The beach you're looking for is right over there."

"The **lighthouse** is there?" Nicky asked.

"Yes, but don't get too close," Kosmas warned them. "I could tell you myths about that place that would make your whiskers **shake**!"

Pam gulped. "Are we sure there are no **GHOSTS**

in there?" she whispered to Paulina.

"Pam, ghosts aren't real. Didn't you hear what Kosmas said? They're just myths. Plus, we'll be together, and Khloe is counting on us!"

Pam took heart at her friend's words. When Kosmas parked the van, she was the first to set out along the steep path toward Big Blue.

At the end of the path was a small, windy beach. The Thea Sisters spotted the old lighthouse at the end of a rocky jetty.

"Let's take a look around. Maybe we'll find some clues," Paulina suggested.

The others nodded and began to search the BEACH.

But after ten minutes, the mouselets gave up. "There's nothing here but shells and seaweed," Nicky said sadly.

Let's go
take a look!

"And rocks!" Pam agreed, hurling a pebble into the sea.

"Guess it's time to check out the most IMPORTANT place," said Violet. She pointed to the lighthouse, which cast a long SHADOW over the sand.

The Thea Sisters cautiously picked their way toward it.

"The door is locked," Paulina said. "What do we do now?"

Then they heard a STRANGE sound. **Thump! Thump!**

The mouselets jumped. It was coming from **inside** the lighthouse!

THE KEY IS IN THE DETAILS

Meanwhile, back in **EPIDAURUS**, the theater company was in the middle of their last rehearsal before opening night. But Khloe couldn't concentrate.

"I have so many things to tell you, I don't know where to start . . ." recited Nikos as Menelaus.

Khloe started to say **Helen's** lines, but then she stopped and **sighed**. "I'm sorry, I can't focus . . . I have too many other things on my mind."

"You need to concentrate! There's only an hour until the **show** begins, and we're about to have a complete cat-astrophe on our paws!" Nestor cried.

Khloe lowered her snout. Her eyes shone with tears.

"Come on, **YOU'LL SEE** — everything will work out . . ." Colette reassured her, placing a paw on her shoulder.

"I'm just so worried about Ioannis," Khloe said.

"Nestor's right," Nikos told her. "We must concentrate on the play. It's our BIG

CHANCE! I've been waiting for this moment for a long time, and now that it's here, we can't let anything ruin it."

Colette shot him a look of surprise and confusion. How could Nikos be thinking of his own **SUCCESS** at a time like this?

She was about to respond when Charissa, the COSTUME assistant, scurried over with an envelope in her paw. "There you are! You're just who I need."

"For what?" Khloe asked.

"To sign this get-well CARD for Melina," Charissa replied. "We got her **flowers**. Poor thing, she's so upset that she's missing opening night."

"What a nice idea," replied Khloe, signing the card.

"How is it going? Is her ankle healing?" asked Colette as Nikos **SIGNED**, too.

Charissa nodded. "Melina will have to **rest** for a few more days, but then she'll be okay."

"Tell her not to worry — we have a **great** understudy here in the meantime!" Khloe said, flashing a warm smile at Colette.

The mouselet blushed, **EMBARRASSED**, and took the card to sign it. Before she gave it back, she glanced at the other *signatures*, and something caught her **ATTENTION**. One of signatures seemed familiar. But why?

Wishing you a speedy recovery!
Your friends,
Nestor Charissa
Nikos
Colette Khloe

What caught Colette's eye?

"The key is in the **details** . . . you just need to look at them the right way . . ." she murmured, remembering what her **friends** had told her. Suddenly, she realized where she'd seen that pawwriting before.

"Colette? Can I have the card back?" Charissa asked, pointing to the **card** in her paws.

"Huh? Oh, yes, of course, sorry!"

"And, Nikos, come with me, please," said Charissa. "The **fur stylist** is waiting to fix your fur like a real **king** of Sparta!"

"Okay, I'm coming," Nikos said. He followed her with a **sigh**.

Colette watched him leave. "Khloe,

do you have **Ioannis's note**? The one that Nestor found the other morning?" she asked.

"Yes, why?"

"Will you show it to me?"

As soon as Colette had the **letter** in her paws, she had no doubt: The pawwriting matched one of the *signatures* she'd seen on Melina's card. It was **NIKOS'S**!

LAST-MINUTE INVESTIGATION!

There was only a half hour until the curtain went up for Helen's opening night.

Colette looked around nervously: Where could Nikos be? She absolutely had to find him and ask him to explain.

The stage was empty, and the first audience members were starting to file in. Colette felt her tail twist with tension as she watched. Soon all these snouts would be turned in her direction . . .

"Keep calm and scurry on," she murmured to herself. "This is no time for stage fright. I need to find Nikos!"

Colette headed to the FUR-STYLING and costume area, but Nikos wasn't there.

"Excuse me, have you **SEEN** Nikos?" she asked the actor closest to her.

"Who commands this strength?" he cried.

"Huh?" said Colette. Before he could reply, an actress explained, "Don't bother him, he's **REHEARSING**. He had to **learn** the part of the messenger Teucer in a ***hurry***, since that was Nikos's part!"

"Squeaking of Nikos," Colette said, "do you know where he is?"

"I think I saw him by the PROPS truck,"

the mouselet replied.

"Thanks!" exclaimed Colette, ***hurrying*** in that direction.

But at the truck there were only two stagehands, who were busy unloading the spotlights.

"Where could he have gone?" Colette muttered. There were only twenty minutes until showtime.

Just then, Colette heard WHISPERING. She followed the sound into a dense cluster of TREES outside the theater. Two figures were standing there.

"I don't understand what you're saying," a **FEMALE** squeak said.

"Khloe, this isn't easy for me . . . This is something I've

wanted to say for a long time, but I couldn't find the **COURAGE**. Now that Ioannis has disappeared without an explanation—"

"Nikos!" Colette interrupted him, stepping of the **SHADOWS**. "You're the one who owes us an explanation!"

"Colette, what are you doing here? Did something happen?" asked Khloe in surprise.

Colette nodded. "I've DISCOVERED something interesting. The note Nestor found wasn't written by Ioannis, was it, Nikos?"

The ratlet turned paler than mozzarella. "What are you saying?"

Colette took a deep breath. "I'm saying that you were the one who wrote it. I recognized your pawwriting!"

Khloe's tail stiffened like a breadstick. "Nikos, is that true?"

"Of course not! I have nothing to do with Ioannis's DISAPPEARANCE. And all this gossip is making us late. The show is about to start!"

Nikos was about to SCURRY AWAY

Stop!

when he was suddenly caught in the glare of two bright lights.

"**STOP!**" cried Pam, scrambling out of Kosmas's van, which had pulled up a few yards from them.

The other THEA SISTERS hurried out after her, with a ratlet right on their tails.

"Ioannis!" Khloe shouted, rushing to **hug** him. "It's you! You're back!"

Ioannis threw his paws around her.

"I was so **worried**! Where have you been?!" Khloe asked.

"I wasn't **far**, but I couldn't get back to you," Ioannis replied.

ALL IS EXPLAINED

Paulina quickly **told** their friends how the mouselets had discovered that Big Blue was the nickname of an abandoned **lighthouse**.

"Uncle Kosmas gave us a **LIFT** out there to look for Ioannis. It took us a while to get the lighthouse door open, but then we found him inside!" Nicky said.

"What were you doing all the way out there?" Khloe asked in **DISBELIEF**.

"Maybe you should ask *him*," Ioannis replied, shooting Nikos a dirty look.

The ratlet lowered his snout. "It's all my fault," he admitted. "I lured Ioannis into a **trap** to keep him away from the theater . . . and from you, Khloe."

"But — but why . . ." the **mouselet** stammered.

"You've always seen me as just a **friend**, but I feel something more for you. You don't know how often I've wanted to tell you. But you only had **EYES** for Ioannis, your Menelaus," Nikos said bitterly.

"And so you tricked me, and trapped me!" Ioannis cried.

"I'm sorry. I wanted to keep you far away on opening night . . . and so I arranged for you to disappear," Nikos said.

"Then you did write that note to Nestor, just as I suspected!" Colette exclaimed.

"Yes, I made up a story about family business, so no one would worry too much about where Ioannis had gone. But I told Ioannis that Nestor needed him to go out to BIG BLUE on an errand."

"And then you locked him in!" Violet concluded.

Nikos nodded. "I didn't want to hurt anyone. I left Ioannis everything he needed: FOOD, water, a blanket for the night . . ."

"I'm just fine, but if it weren't for the Thea Sisters, I would have missed the opening night of our play," Ioannis said.

"And you would have stayed locked away for who knows how long!" cried Khloe in HORROR. "Nikos, what were you thinking?!"

"I was planning to go back and let him out tomorrow . . . Khloe, I wanted to be your leading mouse for just one night!"

Nikos buried his snout in his paws. "I've made a terrible mistake. I didn't mean to make such a mess . . ."

"You should have told Khloe how you felt," Paulina said. "Tricks and LIES never get you what you want."

"I understand that now," Nikos replied sadly, looking at Khloe and Ioannis, who were holding paws HAPPILY.

"What are you all doing out here?!" came

Nestor's squeak from the backstage door. "It's showtime! The audience is **PACKED** in like **SARDINES** in a can! Khloe, Nikos, Ioann — **Ioannis!?** When . . . ? How . . . ?"

"It's a story longer than a cat's tail," Pam said.

"The important thing is that I'm here. And I'm ready to go onstage!" Ioannis said.

THE SHOW MUST GO ON!

There was no time for EXPLANATIONS. Nestor agreed that the roles would return to the way they'd originally been cast: Ioannis would play the part of King Menelaus, and Nikos would be the messenger, Teucer.

"Break a paw, Colette! We'll be ROOTING for you," Pam told Colette. Then she, Nicky, Paulina, and Violet settled into seats in the front row.

Left alone, Colette tried to concentrate on her lines, but she was sure she'd forget everything.

"I can't do it . . . I'm not an actress! This is going to be a CAT-ASTROPHE!" she cried.

Ioannis put a paw around her. "You'll be great! Just **relax** and take deep breaths."

"I can't relax. I'm wound up tighter than a mousetrap spring!"

Ioannis smiled. "That's normal. You just need to turn your nervousness into positive **energy**. Think about something that makes you feel happy . . ."

Colette closed her eyes and tried to follow Ioannis's **ADVICE**. She thought back to a recent evening at Mouseford Academy. The Thea Sisters had an algebra exam the next day, and they'd gotten together for a last-minute **study** session. Violet had fixed everyone a cup of TEA, Pam had passed around a plate of cookies, Nicky had told

funny stories, and Paulina had chosen just the right music.

As she remembered that relaxing evening with her friends, Colette suddenly felt calm. She wasn't alone: She had four special friends who believed in her and were ready to cheer her on.

And so, when it was her turn, Colette scurried onstage excited and full of energy. All she needed was a quick look at her friends in the front row to know that everything was going to be okay.

AFTER THE APPLAUSE

The **PLAY** was a smashing success. Thanks to Ioannis's advice and her friends' support, Colette performed like an expert **actress**. She didn't make a single mistake.

The **best** scene in the show was the reunion of Menelaus and Helen. Ioannis and Khloe **INFUSED** their characters with their own joy at seeing each other again, and it resulted in a scene so **moving**, it blew the audience away!

At the end of the

play, the actors came back onstage so the AUDIENCE could congratulate them and take pictures. The Thea Sisters couldn't wait to take a few snaps of Colette in her costume!

When the crowd had thinned out, Nestor approached Ioannis. "So, is someone going to tell me what happened?!"

Before the ratlet could open his snout, Nikos began squeaking. "It was all my fault, Nestor. I was jealous of Ioannis, and I wanted to play the part of Menelaus with Khloe. So I, er, arranged for his DISAPPEARANCE."

Nikos turned to Ioannis. "I'm so sorry for what I did."

Ioannis lowered his snout. But before he could squeak, Nestor stepped in.

"What you've done is very serious," the

director said sternly. "And not just because you put our play at risk. You mousenapped someone! The actors in this company must trust one another, and I'm afraid I can't trust you after this. So I can't allow you to participate in our company's tour."

"I understand," Nikos replied.

"Wait a minute. What did you say about a tour?!" Khloe cried.

All the actors GATHERED around Nestor, eager to hear their director's BIG announcement.

"That's right, rodents! I'm pleased to say that the world-famouse producer Michael Rattis is sponsoring us on an international tour. Our show isn't just opening in Greece, it will be opening all over EUROPE!"

All the actors cheered.

"Wow!"

We're going on tour!

"That's marvemouse!"

"We're going to perform in the best theaters in the world!"

Nestor **SMILED**. "And there's more. This evening I'm hosting a **cast party**. We'll celebrate by the sea. You're all invited!"

"HOORAY!"

The actors quickly changed out of their costumes and **HEADED** for the beach.

"You're coming, too, right?" said Khloe, clasping Violet's paws.

Violet smiled at her new friend. "Of course we'll come!"

By the time the mouselets REACHED the

seaside, the party was going stronger than Whale Island's annual CheeseFest. There was music, food, and **COLORFUL** decorations to celebrate the success of *Helen* and its cast and crew. It was absolutely fabumouse.

Soon the entire cast and crew was **DANCING** in the moonlight. The Thea Sisters joined Ioannis and Khloe on the dance floor. They were **happy** that opening night had been such a success. And they were prouder than a pack of porcupines that *Colette* had done so well in her acting debut!

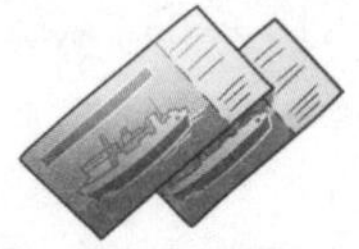

THE SURPRISES AREN'T OVER!

At the end of the party, the Thea Sisters and their new friends **SCAMPERED** back toward Aunt Thalia's inn.

"What a wonderful night!" Paulina commented, looking up at the starry sky.

"Yes, yes, it's beautiful. But there's something I still can't make snouts or tails of," Pam said.

"What's that?" **Violet** asked.

"Oh, it's no big deal, Vi," Pam said hastily. "It's nothing, really . . ."

"Come on, after everything we've been through, squeak what's on your mind," Ioannis urged her.

"All right, Ioannis, if you say so," said Pam.

"Here's what I don't get . . . what is the secret you've been keeping from Khloe?"

Ioannis blushed **REDDER** than a tomato. "What are you talking about?"

"I told the mouselets how you've been acting strange lately," Khloe said. "You're always making mysterious phone calls. I think you've been hiding something!"

Ioannis burst out laughing. "You mouselets are totally on to me! Okay, you've got me. I have no choice but to reveal my secret!"

The mouselets watched Ioannis and waited.

"Khloe, the thing I've been trying to hide from you is . . . a vacation!" Ioannis said.

"What?!" Khloe cried in disbelief.

"Yep, that's it! We've been so tired and

stressed lately, with our busy rehearsal schedule. So I wanted to **SURPRISE** you with a special trip just for us," the ratlet explained. "All those phone calls were to find the **PERFECT** place, and I've finally done it! Just before I disappeared, I bought our boat tickets. Now we'll have a chance to *relax* before the tour begins!"

Khloe **JUMPED UP** and threw her

paws around Ioannis's neck. "This is the best surprise ever!"

"What a great idea, Ioannis!" Colette exclaimed.

"Yeah, that *is* a great IDEA!" Pam put in. "So great that a similar vacation just might be perfect for five FRIENDS who need to relax after solving a major mystery!"

The MOUSELETS burst out laughing. After the adventure they'd had, it was definitely time to enjoy the Greek SEASIDE!

Here, catch!
What a great shot!
How relaxing!

A VERY SPECIAL PERFORMANCE

A few months had passed since the Thea Sisters got back from their exciting trip to **Greece**. I couldn't wait to see them again.

The mouselets returned to Mouseford Academy with more than just **WONDERFUL** memories. They had made a plan: **Helen's** tour would stop on Whale Island! Professor de Mousus was very excited about the chance to introduce his students to the world of Greek drama.

So that **NIGHT**, I put on my elegant red dress and scampered into the **theater** at Mouseford Academy. The headmaster and I couldn't wait to **SEE** Nestor's company at work!

As soon as the lights went out, a hush of suspense fell over the auditorium. When the **curtain** opened, Khloe's squeak filled the entire room. She made a marvemouse Helen!

WATCHING their friends onstage, the **THEA SISTERS** felt as if they were back in Greece again. Colette never took her eyes off Khloe and Ioannis. She even whispered the lines that she had **PRACTICED** so many times.

At the end of the play, there was **thunderous** applause from the audience.

Then Khloe and Ioannis took the stage to say a special **thank-you**. "We dedicate this performance to five special **MOUSELETS** who showed us the meaning of the words friendship, trust, and loyalty. Thank you, Thea Sisters!"

Don't miss these exciting Thea Sisters adventures!

Thea Stilton and the Dragon's Code

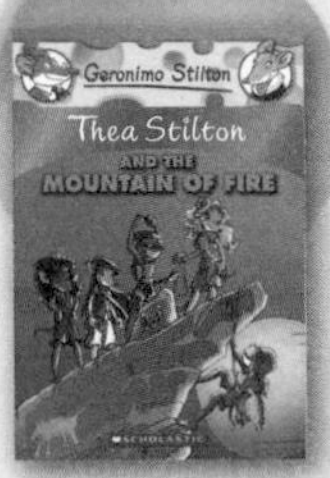

Thea Stilton and the Mountain of Fire

Thea Stilton and the Ghost of the Shipwreck

Thea Stilton and the Secret City

Thea Stilton and the Mystery in Paris

Thea Stilton and the Cherry Blossom Adventure

Thea Stilton and the Star Castaways

Thea Stilton: Big Trouble in the Big Apple

Thea Stilton and the Ice Treasure

Thea Stilton and the Secret of the Old Castle

Thea Stilton and the Blue Scarab Hunt

Thea Stilton and the Prince's Emerald

Thea Stilton and the Mystery on the Orient Express

Thea Stilton and the Dancing Shadows

Thea Stilton and the Legend of the Fire Flowers

Thea Stilton and the Spanish Dance Mission

Thea Stilton and the Journey to the Lion's Den

Thea Stilton and the Great Tulip Heist

Thea Stilton and the Chocolate Sabotage

Thea Stilton and the Missing Myth

Thea Stilton and the Lost Letters

Be sure to read all of our magical special edition adventures!

THE KINGDOM OF FANTASY

THE QUEST FOR PARADISE: THE RETURN TO THE KINGDOM OF FANTASY

THE AMAZING VOYAGE: THE THIRD ADVENTURE IN THE KINGDOM OF FANTASY

THE DRAGON PROPHECY: THE FOURTH ADVENTURE IN THE KINGDOM OF FANTASY

THE VOLCANO OF FIRE: THE FIFTH ADVENTURE IN THE KINGDOM OF FANTASY

THE SEARCH FOR TREASURE: THE SIXTH ADVENTURE IN THE KINGDOM OF FANTASY

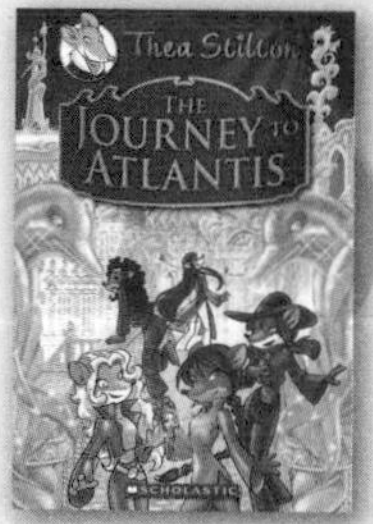

THEA STILTON: THE JOURNEY TO ATLANTIS

THEA STILTON: THE SECRET OF THE FAIRIES

THEA STILTON: THE SECRET OF THE SNOW

Be sure to read all my fabumouse adventures!

#1 Lost Treasure of the Emerald Eye

#2 The Curse of the Cheese Pyramid

#3 Cat and Mouse In a Haunted House

#4 I'm Too Fond of My Fur!

#5 Four Mice Deep in the Jungle

#6 Paws Off, Cheddarface!

#7 Red Pizzas for a Blue Count

#8 Attack of the Bandit Cats

#9 A Fabumouse Vacation for Geronimo

#10 All Because of a Cup of Coffee

#11 It's Halloween, You 'Fraidy Mouse!

#12 Merry Christmas, Geronimo!

#13 The Phantom of the Subway

#14 The Temple of the Ruby of Fire

#15 The Mona Mousa Code

#16 A Cheese-Colored Camper

#17 Watch Your Whiskers, Stilton!

#18 Shipwreck on the Pirate Islands

#19 My Name Is Stilton, Geronimo Stilton

#20 Surf's Up, Geronimo!

#21 The Wild, Wild West

#22 The Secret of Cacklefur Castle

A Christmas Tale

#23 Valentine's Day Disaster

#24 Field Trip to Niagara Falls

#25 The Search for Sunken Treasure

#26 The Mummy with No Name

#27 The Christmas Toy Factory

#28 Wedding Crasher

#29 Down and Out Down Under

#30 The Mouse Island Marathon

#31 The Mysterious Cheese Thief

Christmas Catastrophe

#32 Valley of the Giant Skeletons

#33 Geronimo and the Gold Medal Mystery

#34 Geronimo Stilton, Secret Agent

#35 A Very Merry Christmas

#36 Geronimo's Valentine

#37 The Race Across America

#38 A Fabumouse School Adventure

#39 Singing Sensation

#40 The Karate Mouse

#41 Mighty Mount Kilimanjaro

#42 The Peculiar Pumpkin Thief

#43 I'm Not a Supermouse!

#44 The Giant Diamond Robbery

#45 Save the White Whale!

#46 The Haunted Castle

#47 Run for the Hills, Geronimo!

#48 The Mystery in Venice

#49 The Way of the Samurai

#50 This Hotel Is Haunted!

#51 The Enormouse Pearl Heist

#52 Mouse in Space!

#53 Rumble in the Jungle

#54 Get into Gear, Stilton!

#55 The Golden Statue Plot

#56 Flight of the Red Bandit

The Hunt for the Golden Book

#57 The Stinky Cheese Vacation

#58 The Super Chef Contest

#59 Welcome to Moldy Manor

The Hunt for the Curious Cheese

#60 The Treasure of Easter Island

Don't miss my journeys through time!

Meet GERONIMO STILTONOOT

He is a cavemouse — Geronimo Stilton's ancient ancestor! He runs the stone newspaper in the prehistoric village of Old Mouse City. From dealing with dinosaurs to dodging meteorites, his life in the Stone Age is full of adventure!

#1 The Stone of Fire

#2 Watch Your Tail!

#3 Help, I'm in Hot Lava!

#4 The Fast and the Frozen

#5 The Great Mouse Race

#6 Don't Wake the Dinosaur!

#7 I'm a Scaredy-Mouse!

MEET GERONIMO STILTONIX

He is a spacemouse — the Geronimo Stilton of a parallel universe! He is captain of the spaceship *MouseStar 1*. While flying through the cosmos, he visits distant planets and meets crazy aliens. His adventures are out of this world!

#1 Alien Escape

#2 You're Mine, Captain!

#3 Ice Planet Adventure

#4 The Galactic Goal

Meet
CREEPELLA VON CACKLEFUR

I, *Geronimo Stilton*, have a lot of mouse friends, but none as **spooky** as my friend CREEPELLA VON CACKLEFUR! She is an enchanting and MYSTERIOUS mouse with a pet bat named **Bitewing**. *YIKES!* I'm a real 'fraidy mouse, but even I think CREEPELLA and her family are AWFULLY fascinating. I can't wait for you to read all about CREEPELLA in these fa-mouse-ly funny and **spectacularly spooky** tales!

#1 The Thirteen Ghosts

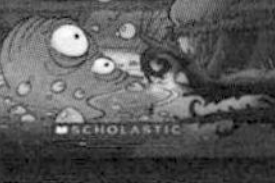

#2 Meet Me in Horrorwood

#3 Ghost Pirate Treasure

#4 Return of the Vampire

#5 Fright Night

#6 Ride for Your Life!

#7 A Suitcase Full of Ghosts

THANKS FOR READING, AND GOOD-BYE UNTIL OUR NEXT ADVENTURE!